Kirby Kelvin and the Not-Laughing Lessons

by Ivon Cecil

pictures by Judy Love

Whispering Coyote Press
Dallas

For David, who believed from the start.
—I.C.

For Kathleen, my dear friend and mentor.
You're always there for me—
in loving appreciation,
—J.D.L.

With special thanks to Dian Curtis Regan and to
the students and faculty, past and present, of
Olsen Park Elementary School in Amarillo,
Texas—I.C.

Published by Whispering Coyote Press
300 Crescent Court, Suite 860, Dallas, TX 75201

Text copyright © 1998 by Ivon Cecil
Illustrations copyright © 1998 by Judith DuFour Love

Text was set in 16-point Garamond 3.
Book production and design by *The Kids at Our House*
10 9 8 7 6 5 4 3 2 1
Printed in Hong Kong

Library of Congress Cataloging–in–Publication Data

Cecil, Ivon, 1954—
Kirby Kelvin and the Not Laughing Lessons / by Ivon Cecil ;
illustrated by Judith DuFour Love.
p.   cm.
Summary: When Kirby gets the giggles during a spelling test, his teacher sends him to
Mr. Gloomsmith for Not–Laughing Lessons.
ISBN 1-879085-95-X (hardcover) ; $14.95,   ISBN 1-879085-39-9 (paperback) ; $5.95
[1. Laughter—Fiction. 2. Behavior—Fiction. 3. Schools—Fiction.]   1. Love, Judith DuFour, ill.   II. Title.
PZ7.C29973K1   1998
[E]—dc21   97–30994
                                                        CIP
                                                        AC

Kirby Kelvin printed his name at the top of his paper. Then he wrote "Spelling Test" on the first line and waited for Ms. Frost to begin.

"Hungry," said Ms. Frost. "The hungry dog ate my cookies."

Kirby Kelvin imagined a skinny dog gobbling cookies out of a cookie jar. Ms. Frost would scold it, and it would run away with the cookie jar stuck on its head. He giggled.

Ms. Frost frowned.

Kirby Kelvin put his hand over his mouth to keep the giggle inside.

"Ugly," said Ms. Frost. "My pet frog is ugly."

Kirby Kelvin imagined a bumpy frog with bulging eyes living in Ms. Frost's desk drawer. It would sit on her shoulder and say, "Ribbit, ribbit," into her ear.

Kirby Kelvin giggled again. He covered his mouth with his hand. The giggle turned into a snort and came out through his nose.

Ms. Frost glared at him over the top of her glasses.

"Today," said Ms. Frost. "I rode my new motorcycle to school today."

Kirby Kelvin imagined Ms. Frost riding a motorcycle in her straight black skirt, ruffled pink blouse, and high-heeled shoes. He giggled until his toes tingled. He laughed so hard, he fell out of his chair and rolled on the floor.

Ms. Frost crossed her arms and tapped her foot. "Kirby Kelvin," she said, "come with me."

Kirby Kelvin followed Ms. Frost as she strode down the hall. Her high heels clicked on the tile floor. He pressed both hands over his mouth, but giggles spilled out like root beer foaming out of a bottle.

Ms. Frost led him to a dim, gray room. A sign on the door read, "Mr. Gloomsmith."

Inside, a gray-looking man in a faded gray suit sat behind a gray desk.

"Kirby Kelvin needs Not-Laughing Lessons," said Ms. Frost.

"Very well." Mr. Gloomsmith pointed to a chair. "Sit there, young man." Even his voice sounded gray.

Kirby Kelvin's giggles disappeared. He sat in a cold metal chair at a cold metal desk.

Ms. Frost frowned one more time before she left.

"Let us begin," said Mr. Gloomsmith. "Close your eyes."
Kirby Kelvin closed his eyes. "Think about all your friends
riding new bicycles," said Mr. Gloomsmith. "Red bicycles,
green bicycles, silver bicycles.

But you have to ride an *old* bicycle. A bicycle
as old as your grandfather. A rusty, creaky,
squeaky bicycle."

Kirby Kelvin thought about riding a
rusty, creaky, squeaky bicycle. The corners
of his mouth drooped.

"Think about building
a tree house," said Mr.
Gloomsmith. "You work
all summer.

Then your little sister falls out of it and bumps her head. Your father makes you tear down the tree house." Kirby Kelvin thought about tearing down his tree house. His shoulders sagged.

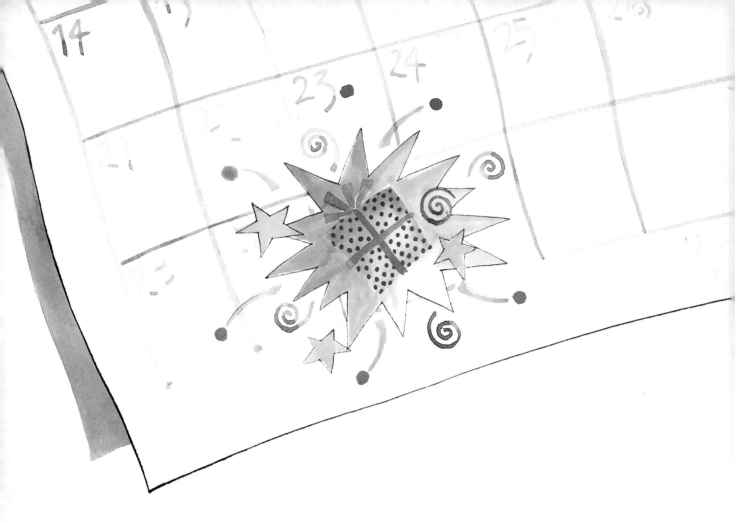

"Think about your next birthday," said Mr.
Gloomsmith. "What if everyone forgets? What if
you have a birthday with no party? No presents?
No one singing 'Happy Birthday to You'?"

Kirby Kelvin thought about everyone forgetting
his birthday. It made him so sad he had to open
his eyes.

"Mr. Gloomsmith, don't you ever think of anything happy? Don't you ever laugh?"

Mr. Gloomsmith leaned over Kirby Kelvin's desk. "Young man, I haven't laughed in twenty-nine years. I don't even remember how."

Kirby Kelvin couldn't imagine not remembering how to laugh.

"That's terrible!" he cried. "I have an idea, Mr. Gloomsmith. Close your eyes."

"Humph." Mr. Gloomsmith folded his arms across his chest. But he did close his eyes.

"Think about riding a creaky, squeaky, old bicycle," said Kirby Kelvin.

"You could clean off the rust. Then you could paint it red and green and silver all mixed together

and tie streamers to the handlebars.

Then all your friends would watch you race down the street and wish for bicycles like yours."

Mr. Gloomsmith snorted. "Silliness and nonsense!"

Kirby Kelvin tried again. "Think about tearing down your tree house. You could use the pieces to make a cage for your little sister. Then you could build another tree house better than the first one."

Mr. Gloomsmith shook his head. "Silliness and nonsense!"

Kirby Kelvin swallowed hard. "Think about everyone forgetting your birthday. You could bake yourself a cake with chocolate icing and rainbow sprinkles. You could give yourself a mountain of presents and sing 'Happy Birthday to Me'."

Mr. Gloomsmith opened his eyes. "Silliness and nonsense!" he said. "Enough!"

Kirby Kelvin took a deep breath.

"Think about Ms. Frost in her straight black
skirt, ruffled pink blouse, and high-heeled shoes.
Think about her riding a motorcycle to school."

Mr. Gloomsmith opened his mouth. He closed it again. The corners twitched into a smile. His shoulders began to shake. He gave a rusty chuckle. He cackled a creaky cackle. He threw back his head and laughed.

He laughed so hard his whole body swayed back and forth.
He laughed so hard he had to sit on the floor and hold his sides.

Finally, he pulled out a handkerchief and wiped his
eyes. "Thank you, Kirby Kelvin. Thank you for helping me
remember how to laugh."

Kirby Kelvin and Mr. Gloomsmith went to Ms. Frost's room. School was over and everyone was going home.

"Kirby Kelvin has finished his Not-Laughing Lessons," said Mr. Gloomsmith.

"I hope he will know how to behave tomorrow," said Ms. Frost.

Kirby Kelvin nodded. "Yes ma'am, I will."

"Good." Ms. Frost opened her closet, took out her leather jacket, and slipped it on. She lifted a helmet off the top shelf.

Kirby Kelvin stared.

Mr. Gloomsmith raised his eyebrows.

"Good-bye," said Ms. Frost, whisking out the door. The sound of her high heels clicking on the tile grew faint and disappeared.

Kirby Kelvin and Mr. Gloomsmith rushed to the window.
They watched Ms. Frost zip away on a brand-new black-and-
silver motorcycle in her straight black skirt, ruffled pink
blouse, and high-heeled shoes. And they laughed until their
toes tingled.